EXPLORERS OF THE WILD

CALE ATKINSON

DISNEY • HYPERION / Los Angeles New York

I love to explore!

It's my *favorite* thing to do!

There are so many neat things to see.
Like over there!

And so many strange things to find...
Like under here!

My parents tell me to be careful.

They say you never know what you'll run into in the **wild**.

I say I'm an explorer,

So I climb over trees.

I roll down hills.

I run
and
I run

until
one day
I ran
right into...

I mean I was really **scared,** but then...

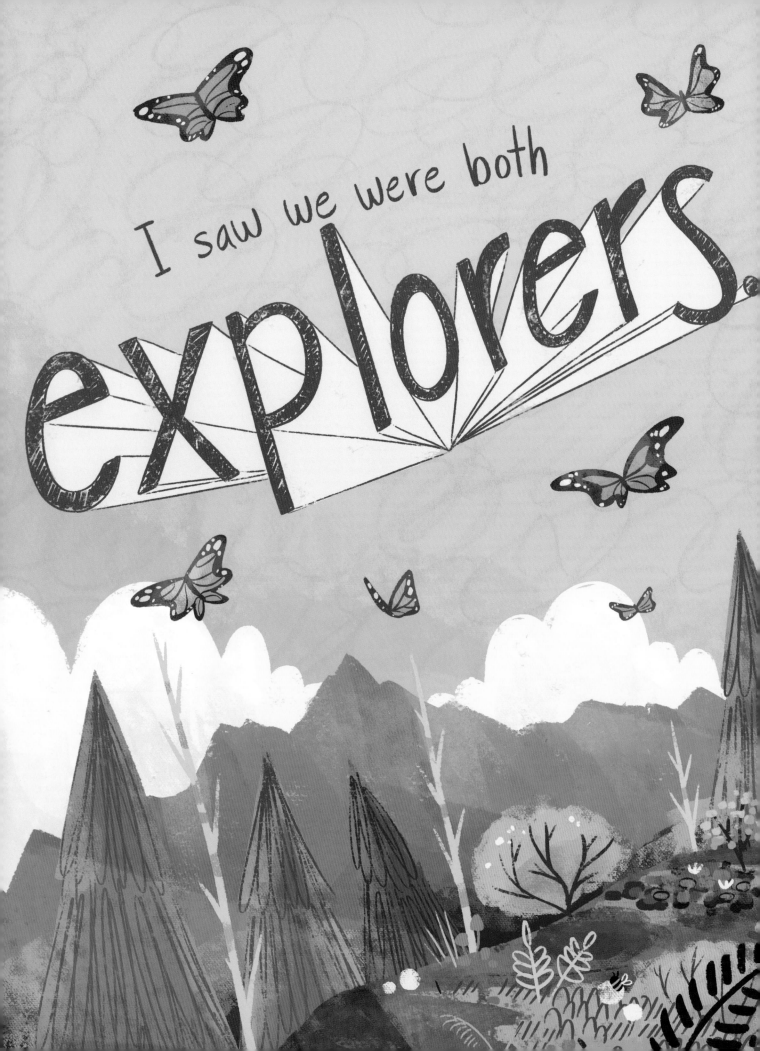

I saw we were both explorers.

Together, we found things to touch,

things to see,

things to hear,

and even things to taste... well, kind of.

and no mountain was too big to **conquer.**

This was our day.

This was our adventure.

We were **kings** of the **wild.**

but I had
to go
home.

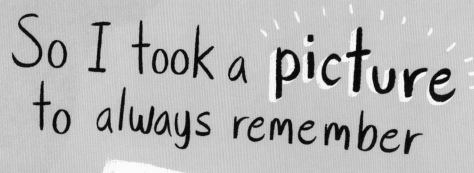

So I took a **picture**
to always remember

Dedicated to every explorer
who runs through the wild
with an open mind,
and an open heart

Printed in Malaysia
Reinforced binding

First Edition, April 2016
10 9 8 7 6 5 4 3 2 1
FAC-029191-16032

Library of Congress Cataloging-in-Publication Data

Atkinson, Cale, author, illustrator.
  Explorers of the wild / Cale Atkinson.—First edition.
    pages cm
  Summary: "A bear and a boy who both love exploring learn to share
their adventures together"—Provided by publisher.
  ISBN 978-1-4847-2340-1—ISBN 1-4847-2340-6
  [1. Play—Fiction. 2. Explorers—Fiction. 3. Adventure and
adventurers—Fiction. 4. Bears—Fiction.] I. Title.
  PZ7.A86372Ex 2016
  [E]—dc23   2015011770

Visit www.DisneyBooks.com